Book Club Edition

WALT DISNEY PRODUCTIONS
presents

Christmas in the Country

Random House 🏠 **New York**

First American Edition. Copyright © 1982 by Walt Disney Productions. All rights reserved under International and Pan-American Copyright Conventions. Published in the United States by Random House, Inc., New York, and simultaneously in Canada by Random House of Canada Limited, Toronto. Originally published in Denmark as JUL PAA LANDET by Gutenberghus Gruppen, Copenhagen. ISBN: 0-394-85876-X. Manufactured in the United States of America   2 3 4 5 6 7 8 9 0   A B C D E F G H I J K

It was the day before Christmas.

Donald Duck's nephews were out shopping.

"Wow, look at that big Christmas tree!" said Huey.

"I wonder how big our tree at Grandma's house will be," said Dewey.

"Hey, we have to make the decorations for it," said Louie. "Let's go home."

Donald Duck was at work in the office
of his rich uncle, Scrooge McDuck.

Donald saw that it was starting to snow.
He hoped Uncle Scrooge would
let him leave early.

Donald took his hat and
went to see Scrooge.

"What? Leave early? Of course not!"
said Scrooge McDuck.

"But, Uncle, tomorrow is Christmas," said
Donald. "I want to go home and get ready.
We are all going to Grandma Duck's farm
for the day. Why don't you come too?"

"Christmas? Bah, humbug!" said Scrooge.
"I have no time for Christmas. Now get
back to your desk!"

What a hustle and bustle there was over at Donald's house!

Daisy Duck mixed dough for cookies.

Huey cut up colored paper to make paper chains.

Louie painted a design on a box for the cookies.

Dewey made some paper hearts.

Then he rolled up paper to make paper cones.

Next the boys helped
to make the cookies.

Louie rolled out the dough.

Huey made long sticks of dough
and twisted them into curly cookies.

Dewey cut out
round shapes with
a cookie cutter.

And Daisy put the cookies
in the oven to bake.

Donald got home late.
"Hooray! Here's Uncle Donald!"
shouted the boys.

"Why are you boys still up?" Donald asked. "You should be in bed by now."

"We have to show you what we made," said the boys.

They held up their decorations.

"Beautiful!" said Donald. "Grandma will be pleased."

"Off to bed now, boys," said Donald.
"We have to get an early start tomorrow."

"Look, it's still snowing," said Huey as the boys climbed into bed.

"I hope it snows a lot," said Dewey.

"White Christmases are the best," said Louie.

All night long it snowed
and snowed and snowed.

The boys woke up at dawn.

"WOW!" said Huey. "Look at all the snow!"

Snow covered yards and walks and fences and bushes.

It even covered Uncle Donald's car.

"Come on, let's get dressed," said Dewey.

"Let's dig out the car for Uncle Donald," said Louie. "Or we'll be late to Grandma's house."

"The shovels are in the basement," said Huey.

When the boys opened the door, a pile
of snow fell into the house.

"My goodness, this is going to be
a big job," said Huey.

First the boys shoveled the walk.
Then they started to work on the car.
Dewey brushed snow off the windows and roof.
Huey and Louie dug all around the car.

"Let's take our skis and sled and
snowshoes," said Dewey. "We can play
in the snow at Grandma's."

By the time Donald and Daisy were ready
to leave, the car was all ready too.

"Good work, boys," said Donald.

They set off through the snowy streets.
"Drive carefully, Donald," said Daisy.
"You bet," said Donald. "But don't worry.
I'm the world's best driver!"
He drove slowly through town.

Soon they were out in the country.
The snow was even deeper there.

"Hey, look! Uncle
Scrooge's house is
over there," said
Huey. "Why don't we
stop and wish him a
Merry Christmas?"

"Good idea!" said Donald.
He put on the brakes and
gave the steering wheel
a sharp turn . . .

... and the car skidded into a bank of snow!

"This car is really stuck," said Daisy.
"How are we ever going to get to Grandma's?"

"Uncle Scrooge has a sleigh and horses,"
said Donald. "But the snow is too deep
to walk in. How can we reach him?"

"I know!" said Huey.

He climbed up on top of the car.

"We can use our skis and snowshoes and sled! They'll take us to Uncle Scrooge's house!"

The boys set off.

"Don't worry," called Louie. "We'll be back in no time. Uncle Scrooge will help us."

"I'm not so sure about that," said Donald to Daisy. "Scrooge thinks Christmas is humbug."

A giant snowdrift went up to Scrooge's
bedroom window.

"Let's give Uncle Scrooge a surprise,"
said Louie.

He led the way up the mountain of snow.

Scrooge was sitting happily in bed.

He was adding up how much money he had made during the year.

Suddenly he heard a tapping at the window.

He looked up and saw his nephews.

"What on earth?" he squawked.

Scrooge leaped out of bed and threw open the window.

"What do you think you are doing?" he yelled.

"Uh—Merry Christmas, Uncle Scrooge," said Huey.

Huey climbed in the window and said, "We came to ask your help, Uncle Scrooge. Our car is stuck in a snowbank and we can't get to Grandma's for Christmas."

"Bah!" said Scrooge.

He looked at the three sad little faces.

"Oh, all right," said Scrooge. "I'll see what I can do."

And he pulled on his clothes.

Scrooge stepped out
onto the snowdrift and
closed the window.
"Might as well leave
the easy way," he said.

Then Scrooge hopped on the sled with
Huey and—WHEEE!—they slid down the hill.
Scrooge almost smiled.

Scrooge and the boys went to the stables.
Inside they found a gleaming sleigh and
four eager horses.

Scrooge hitched up the four horses,
and the boys piled into the sleigh.

"Harrumph!" Scrooge
said. "Just a minute.
We might as well do
things properly!"

He found an axe
and chopped down
a beautiful fir tree.

Then he dragged the tree over to
the sleigh.
"Oh, Grandma
will love it!"
said the boys.

Donald and Daisy were getting colder and colder.

But suddenly they heard the sound of jingle bells.

Here came Scrooge driving the sleigh!

"Hooray!" said Daisy.

"I don't believe it!" said Donald.

Everyone helped unload the car and load up the sleigh.

Then off they went to Grandma's house.
The jingle bells rang merrily as
the horses trotted down the road.

It started to snow again, but no one
minded a bit.

Finally they got to Grandma's.
Grandma rushed outside and called,
"Hello, hello! I'm so glad to see you.
I never thought you'd make it through
the snow! Why, my goodness, if it isn't
Scrooge McDuck! Merry Christmas!"

Daisy and the boys brought in the presents
while Donald and Scrooge carried in the tree.

"Come in and have
some hot cocoa,"
said Grandma. "You
must be frozen!"

When the boys were
warm again, Dewey
unpacked the paper chains.

Louie brought out
the paper hearts and
cones.

And Huey opened
a box of glass balls.

Then the boys
trimmed the tree.
"It's beautiful!"
said Grandma.

Soon it was time for Christmas dinner.
"What a wonderful meal!" said Donald.

"Thanks to Grandma," said Daisy, "and
also thanks to Uncle Scrooge. Without
his help we wouldn't even be here."

"Hooray for Grandma and Uncle Scrooge!"
yelled Huey, Dewey, and Louie.

"Thank you," said Scrooge.
"And Merry Christmas to you!"